Lavender and Pearls

Where Pearls are Keys to Magical Worlds
Sue Carpenter

Sue Carpenter

Contents

"Just because it doesn't make sense –
doesn't mean it isn't so."

Dedication

Dedicated to Frankie – My 12-year-old who reminds me children like to look at the clouds.

Dedicated to Lucas – who questions what needs to be questioned.

Dedicated to Marco – without him we would never leave the house on time.

Friday April 8th

'**D**ear Diary,' Hayden uses a mock female voice.

'Give it back,' I scream, jumping for him.

'Today's a hard day 'cause I went for a walk past a lavender bush,' he carries on reading in his put-on '*me*' voice.

'Stop,' I half scream – half beg.

'Jackie, what's lavender?' He asks in his normal tone.

'A flower. Please don't read any more,' I reply calmly.

He sits up on the banister of my bedroom and goes silent as he reads more. I can never climb like him – he's a little monkey. I don't want him to read my diary – not because of him teasing me, but because I don't want to upset him. He handles it all better than I – because he's only nine and doesn't remember her as clearly as I do.

I started writing in diaries when Mum first disappeared to show her when she came home. But it's been years. I guess she's not coming home.

'Mum?' he whispers.

'Please don't read,' I beg again.

'This is all about Mum? Did she like lavender?' he asks.

'She always smelt of it'

'What does it smell like?'

'Come,' I reach out for him. I don't know how to describe the smell – like a dream, a memory, relaxing and magical.

He throws the pink and purple glittery diary down to me, then scurries, following it. Hand in hand, we walk out the front door and down the road a few blocks. I stop under a large gum tree. A lavender hedge runs along the front of the orange brick house. I pick a flower and pass it to Hayden.

He inhales. 'Oh, oh yes,' he says sniffing the flower.

I pick myself a flower, too, and we walk back home in silence, well, aside from the constant white noise of Sydney's expressway.

As we walk down our paved driveway, Dad pulls in. He turns the car off and stretches out of his golden Holden. 'G'day kids, how was the last day of term?' He walks to the passenger side of his car and takes out his laptop bag.

'Hey,' we both say before walking to greet him with a family hug.

'What's that?' Dad asks, looking around. 'Nell?' he whispers Mum's name.

'We got some flowers,' Hayden says, opening his palm to show the small purple flower.

'Oh,' Dad closes his eyes, inhaling the sweet, woodsy smell. 'Your mother believed weird things about lavender – she would get so worried if she didn't have some close by. Come inside, we need to chat.' Dad lifts Hayden onto his shoulders, his work bag under his right arm, and I snuggle in under his left.

We walk inside, Hayden ducking at the doorway, and step through to the kitchen. Dad opens the oven and sees the lasagna I made after school while Hayden was mon-keying around. Hayden slides down Dad's back, and I pour three glasses of water –

carrying them to the table. My brother and I add our lavender to the vase of flowers in the middle of the table and sit.

I look up at the large portrait on the wall. The four of us, mum, dad, son and daughter. Were we a perfect family? Mum disappeared the weekend after it was taken, and she never saw the finished product. Her long, fine, blonde – almost white hair – was perfectly straight, while the rest of us have hair so curly you can hardly run a comb through it. Yet somehow, my brother and I are a perfect combination of our parents. Our faces and eyes are like hers – just darker. As fair as Mum was, Dad's the opposite.

Dad takes the lasagna out of the oven and carries it to the table. I dish out the salad as he divides up the pasta.

'Kids, sorry, but I have to go away for work for a week.'

'What about us?' Hayden asks.

'I can look after him if you stock the kitchen with food,' I say. I basically do it all, anyway.

'You are only fourteen, and as amazing as you are, it's illegal.' Dad says.

I knew this day would come. Dad goes away twice a year for work, and we had always stayed with his Mum, Golli, but she died eight months ago, leaving us with no other family.

'I'm going to New Zealand, and I've arranged for you to stay with an aunty over there.'

'We don't have any aunties,' I say.

'You do. She's from your mother's side.'

'Why don't we know her?'

'You did when you were younger. We had a lot of trouble with your Aunty Claire when your mum first went missing. She kept breaking into the house at nighttime. She moved here to help find your mum, but she didn't help me with you. I don't know what she did, but she left a year later and has lived all over the world. She never stays in one place longer than a year.'

'How do you keep in contact with her?' I ask, not ever remembering a birthday card or Christmas gift from an aunty.

'She emails me every Tuesday to see if your mother has come home. I wish I had her faith.'

'So, you think she is crazy and are sending us to stay with her?'

'She's not crazy – just umm crazy.'

'Thanks for clearing that up! When are we going?' I ask Dad.

Sheepishly, he looks up at the ceiling.

'Dad,' I use my adult voice.

'I was too scared to tell you.'

'When are we going, Dad?' Hayden asks.

'Tomorrow, we have an early morning flight.'

'Dad, we need passports. We need to pack. We can't be ready by then.' What's wrong with him? Telling us at the last moment.

'I have your passports sorted. I'm already packed. I'll do the dishes. You guys go pack.'

My chair falls over when I shove it towards the table.

Hayden says nothing and wanders down the narrow hall to his room.

I want to stomp off in a huff, but Hayden is in my way. However, I can still slam the door, and I do □ so hard that a framed photo falls off my wall. The picture is one of Mum holding me when I was a baby. The protective glass is wet from my tears. Slowing my breathing, I dry off the frame and place it back on its hook, glad the glass isn't broken. What should I take to New Zealand? I think it's colder there than in Australia. Long sleeve tops with tights. Tomorrow I'll wear my jeans and a hoodie.

I zip up my packed bag and go to help Hayden. To my surprise, Dad is with him, and they have packed together. Hayden is snuggled next to Dad, reading him a book about rocket ships, planets, and comets.

This wasn't how I planned my school holidays. I leave them to it, crawl into bed, put my audiobook on with a timer to go off after half an hour. Thinking I will never fall asleep.

Saturday April 9th

Next thing I know, Dad is turning my light on, saying, 'It's time to go, Jelly-bean.'

I hadn't even heard the audiobook finish. Quickly, I take a shower and get dressed. In the dining room, breakfast is on the table – that's a job I've always done. Dad's on his laptop as normal, but for him to make breakfast, he must be feeling guilty. I wonder if my Aunty will make breakfast. Will she mother us? Do I want to be mothered? What if she makes us eat weird New Zealand food? What if we have thousands of annoying noisy cousins running around? 'Dad, do we have any cousins?'

'Do we?' Hayden asks in his hyperactive voice.

'No. Not that I know of.'

'What do you mean, not that you know of?'

'We need to go, now.' Dad looks at his watch – it's his way of getting out of answering us. We put our dishes in the dishwasher and climb into his car.

The drive to the airport is half an hour in early morning traffic. Dad parks his car in the long-term car park. With our bags, we tread the concrete walk to the terminal. Dad does our travel paperwork, and then we pass through customs. I have to tip out my drink bottle. It's so annoying, especially as it's my favourite, Raspberry Cottees.

'I'll get you a fizzy raspberry drink,' Dad promises. But we are running late and have to go straight to the gate.

The flight to Wellington is three hours with no drink. They have water and tea. Double disgusting. Hopefully, they have raspberry cordial over the ditch.

As soon as we process through customs in New Zealand, a lady comes rushing over to us. I freeze, looking at her. She's almost my mother. Her hair has a tinge of apricot in it, and she looks older than Mum. It's years since we've seen Mum. She'll be older now

– if she's alive. The police say that seeing she was such a loving mum and there was no trace of her, we shouldn't keep our hopes up.

Aunty Claire puts her arms out to hug me, but I move away. She looks normal enough in a flowing white dress that looks a hundred years old and a lace handbag. Three sets of pearls around her neck, aside from that, no twitching eye or anything.

'Thanks, Claire,' Dad says before he quickly kisses us. He runs off towards the car park, phone connected to his ear.

'Dad,' Hayden calls, but Dad doesn't look back. I place my hand on Hayden's shoulder, knowing just how it feels. Dad loves us. He just forgets to show us from 7 am till 7 pm.

'Well – I have somewhere fun places to explore. Do you like dinosaurs?' Aunty Claire asks as Dad disappears out of sight.

'Oh yes,' Hayden says, jumping up and down.

Well, he got over Dad fleeing quickly. Hayden always bounces back. I don't! We follow our aunty. As I watch her, I see she has different characteristics than I remember Mum having, however most of my mum memories are only from my dreams. Aunty is taller and comes across as fragile. On edge, she rushes us into her large, empty van.

All three of us squeeze in the front. The inside looks like someone has hastily cleaned it, but it's still messy. I see chocolate wrappers wedged between the seats. How dirty will her house be?

Hayden chats away nonstop to the lady – our aunty.

She points out the harbour and sculptures. We have a harbour and sculptures in Sydney – so what! I would prefer to look at the clouds and make shapes in them.

We arrive at a large building on the waterfront, and Aunty Claire stops. 'Take these with you.' She hands us an envelope each. 'But don't open them.' Then she gives us both a green note – $20 and says, 'Meet me back here in two hours.' She revs her engine and drives off.

'Did she seriously just dump us?' I ask, 'And paid us $20 for the effort?'

'I'll have yours if you don't want it?' Hayden lifts his envelope to the sun. 'I can't see what it is. But that smell.'

I take a sniff. 'It's lavender and feels like lots of round marbles.' Dad warned us Aunty Claire was weird and not to listen to her insane beliefs. 'Maybe she's a witch?'

'She sure is jumpy. Come on ☐ let's find dinosaurs.' I follow my jumping brother into the museum and grab a map while he bounces around, excited at a spinning water wheel.

Up some large stairs we find a theatre. A show starts, led by a man with the biggest frizzy hair I've ever seen. The man sings and tells stories to a crowd of eager children, his voice reaching every octave. Before I can stop Hayden, he hops over and joins in, singing and chanting along with the crowd. I stand next to the other mothers. At least this will kill a little time. As soon as the show finishes, I send Hayden off to the toilet, then feed him, taking opportunistic bites of my sandwich, too. I follow him in a rushed walk past large plastic dinosaurs to an earthquake room, looking at bugs and birds till we find a kids' exploring area, and Hayden heads off to discover.

'Hi,' a boy around my age comes up to me as I lean against a wall.

'Hey,' he says.

'Hi?'

'Look,' he turns both our faces to a kaleidoscope where we can see his face and mine so many times I can't count. He laughs, but my nose crinkles at him. Is he four or fourteen?

'Gee, do you know how to have fun?'

'Fun?'

'Relax a bit, bro,' he says.

'Bro? I'm a girl!'

He grabs my hand and runs me to an area with small, dotted lights moving around a wall.

'Touch as many blue ones as you can,' he says.

'It's just a projector with lights,' I roll my eyes.

'Relax and let loose.' He jumps around, touching blue ones, acting like a child.

Hayden comes over. 'What's the game?'

'Touch the blue ones, bro,' the boy says. The two of them jump around, chasing blue dots like kittens following laser lights. When they are puffed and laughing too hard to jump any more, they come back to me.

'Are you related to her?' the boy asks.

'Sister.'

'Does she ever chill?'

'No,' Hayden replies.

'I read a book last night,' I defend myself.

'Ohhhh,' the boy sing.

'Live a little beanie,' Hayden taunts, spinning around with his arms wide open. Smash. An antique vase shatters into pieces on the ground. Hayden bloody knocked it over, and staff are running towards us. Nowhere to hide.

'It's been fun,' the local says before he disappears.

'That's why I don't get to have fun.' I say under my breath, getting ready to try to parent my way out of another Haydensituation.

We leave the museum after too many *'Why don't you have a guardian or an adult's phone number'* conversations with the security team and before they call the police.

I sit at the waterfront, looking at the harbour while Hayden chases seagulls. The antique van shows up ten minutes early. We run over and jump in. There is a wooden antique wardrobe tied up in the back of the van and a white piano stool with maroon and gold stripes.

'Did you guys have a great time?' she asks.

'It sure was interesting,' I say.

'History's always interesting.' She doesn't pick up on my sarcasm.

We drive ten minutes in the van, pull into a car park, and Aunty Claire gets out, beckoning for us to follow. We walk next door to the zoo.

Hayden's eyes light up, but mine just roll again. She buys tickets for the three of us, and we walk in, but then she turns to me and says, 'I should be back in an hour.' She hightails it, leaving us another $20 each. I now have $40.

The zoo is so confusing because you can't start on one path and follow it around to the finish. It is like a choose-your-own-adventure book. You choose this path, but you'll miss out on the bears. Or choose the bear path and miss out on the giraffes, but in the end, we miss nothing. Hayden runs up and down all the paths, looking at every animal for one minute before moving on to another. Shame I'm not training for cross-country –

this is the perfect place to practise. The hills go up and down, the paths all around, and it takes us an hour till the end. Hayden is even a little bit worn out.

We get ice blocks at the cafe and wait outside for ages; she's late. Finally, she arrives, more on edge – and people call me uptight. Maybe it's a family thing. This time, she doesn't even have time to ask. Hayden starts throwing facts at her about the great time he'd had. I have to smile at that. Nothing broken – thank goodness. I see something move from the corner of my eye. I turn to the back of the van. There is a bronze lamp on a stand the height of Hayden, tied to the wall, and a Harry Potter-type chest that looks like it's waiting to board a steam train to a magical world, furniture, and also a man wearing a black suit and white shirt with a black tie. His skin is a shade of grey, and it's all topped off with a black bowler hat. He almost looks like a cartoon. He taps his hand twice over his heart and then points at me.

'Aunty Claire?' I say.

'Don't interrupt your brother,' she says. When I turn back, the man is gone. Maybe

I have jet lag? Seeing things. I keep looking around for him until we stop outside a mall.

I choose to have Sushi for lunch. It tastes the same as at home. Aunty Claire even joins us for ten minutes before she says we can have twenty minutes of looking around the mall. She gives us another $20 each. I buy a crunchie bar but still want a raspberry drink, so I walk around the mall looking for one. Hayden buys a bag full of munchies, chippies, and lollies. He's down to $20. The day's wasting away on being tourists.

When Aunty Claire shows up next, the stress lines on her face are highlighted. If I knew her better, I would ask to help her, but she's abandoned us at tourist desti-nations all day, so I don't care. We drive over a big hill and finally out of Wellington. Hayden quickly falls asleep and misses a view, which I have to say is spectacular as we drive down. There is a perfectly formed island surrounded by a turquoise sea.'

'That's Kapiti Island. There are wild kiwis over there, Jacquelin.'

'You can call me Jackie.' I've just seen kiwis at the zoo, and there's nothing special about their national bird. Our emu – now that's a bird worth talking about!

'Do you know what colour the sand is at the beach down there?'

'White.' How dumb, or young does she think I am?

'Black.'

'Really?' No way there is black sand. This lady sure is crazy.

'See those?' Aunty points to some islands in the far distance north-west of where we are. 'That's the South Island,' she says. I know that New Zealand is made up of two main islands; it doesn't seem right that the South Island is north of me when I am on the North Island.

The next town we come to, we stop again. Hayden wakes as we pull into a large yet empty car park. His eyes pop at the car museum sign. Is this lady trying to kill me with boredom? I ask Aunty. 'How long are we here for?' She doesn't pick up the bitterness in my voice.

'Do you think they will have Lamborghinis?' Hayden interrupts.

'Only half an hour. I'll be back soon.' Another $20 is shoved at us each. Today has cost her a fortune just in the money she offloads to us.'

Bet they have McLarens. Bruce McLaren was from New Zealand.'

Before we climb out, I look in the back. No man. I must have been having a moment. Hayden runs ahead to the car museum; his favourite car, an old Mercedes Benz, is at the entrance. The gift shop has a Mercedes T-shirt, so he buys the tee. The most interesting car I see is a gangster Cadillac with bullet holes. There's even a jet there. I suppose this place isn't as bad as I worried it might be, and I love the fact that we get around without Hayden being too Hayden-ish.

When we leave, Aunty's already there, pacing up and down, running her hand through her pearls.

'Are you alright?' I ask her.

'Oh yes, fine, fine. Only one more stop, and then we'll be home.'

The day's almost over. I check the back again; it's getting packed in there. Not a lot of room for a man now, which sets my mind at ease. There was something scary about him. His hand on his heart like that. Did he want my heart or love me? I don't believe in ghosts, but if I did, I would think he was an ancestor, great, great something-or-other. We drive another twenty minutes and pull into a small town with a large windmill.

'This is Foxton. There's not a lot to do here, sorry. You can look at the flour mill, and they do the most incredible fizzy drinks.' Another $20, and the van disappears around a corner. I've made over $60. The tour of the mill is...different. Mini clogs and tea-towels, nothing to waste cash on. We walk into the dairy, where they sell Foxton Fizz. A raspberry-flavoured fizzy drink. I'm so excited to finally get my raspberry fix.

'How do you open it?' I ask the lady. It has a tin cap on its glass neck.

'Just put the palm of your hand on it and twist.'

Hayden orders a lime one, and he's drinking his before I've even opened mine. 'It's amazing,' he says.

I slowly sip. It's the best raspberry drink I've ever tasted; I savour it with each drop. No, it's the best any-flavoured drink. Amazing. The raspberry is sweet and delicious. It doesn't quench my thirst. It makes me want more and more. On my third swig, I ask the lady, 'Can you buy these all over New Zealand?'

'No, they are from a boutique factory, so only select places sell them.'

'Can I please buy a box?' I will have a raspberry Foxton Fizz every day that I'm in New Zealand. No matter how horrible being abandoned is, the fizz will help. Aunty pulls up in the van. 'Quick, quick – get in,' she says in a panic. When Aunty Claire calms down, she asks 'what's withe the box?'

I tell her about my love for raspberry drinks.

She laughs 'Raspberry was your mother's favourite drink.' I didn't know that. It was nice to learn something about Mum. Hayden hangs on every word anybody ever says about Mum. He'd been too young to remember her.

We arrive in a dinky town, which has cow statues everywhere. We pull into the McDonald's drive-through. It's almost the same as Australia, except they have something called a Kiwi burger. Hayden and I each buy that, and we drive across the main road. We instantly turn left onto a gravel driveway behind a set of shops. Aunty Claire parks outside a tall and wide brick building. No carport or garage.

We jump out of the car and get our luggage from her boot. Every garden space we can see has lavender plants growing in it.

'More pork,' comes a noise from the darkness right by Hayden.

I jump as Aunty laughs. 'That's just the call of our native owl – ruru. Some people call it a morepork.'

Hayden laughs, 'I will call it a morepork.'

I don't laugh, 'Well, I will call it a ruru because that's its name. Imagine if we started calling cats meow or if dogs became woofs, and what would we call a giraffe? No one even knows what noise they make.'

We climb outdoor stairs to get to the top floor, where there are four wooden doors surrounded by brick.

'Which one is yours?' Hayden asks.

She points to the one on the right-hand side.

'Who lives in the others?' He asks.

'The two right ones are also mine – the others are currently vacant. Normally, we have a string of students renting them.'

We walk through the threshold of the little brick flat into a world of elegance. The chairs and couches all have little engraved wooden claw feet. Two walls are filled with paintings and photos in elegant gold frames. All the furniture and even the wallpaper looks majestic. The maroon curtains ruffle and spread out around the walls of the room. We sit at an elaborate dining table and chairs with embossed flowers and eat MacDonalds out of bags in silence. I am still taking the space in and chewing. From the outside, this place looks like a dinky flat. What a transformation.

'It's late, bedtime,' Aunty Claire says. She shows Hayden to a room with an enormous bed in the centre. Navy and mint velvet bedding, with more pillows than I've ever seen in my life. I want to complain, but not knowing Aunty Claire well enough, I decide to leave it. I know she is French. Maybe in France, boys get bigger and more elaborate beds. In Aussie, as the oldest, I should've had it.

Hayden does a big running jump into the middle of the bed and laughs. He looks at me and says, 'It'll do.'

Aunty Claire laughs. That's a good sign, as she hasn't shown much personality until now.

Hayden leaves his bag on an antique chest of drawers beside his pillow pile and walks out, flicking a set of pearls hanging over the door handle. I remember Mum had a thing for pearls; always wore them and had them hanging in weird spots around the house. She gave me pearls when I was young. I haven't seen them for years. I wonder if Dad has put them away somewhere for me.

We walk into another bedroom, like Hayden's room. It also has pearls on the door handle. My body relaxes as I see the room in its entirety.

Hayden laughs. 'This room is perfect for you.' It has a carved wooden four-posted bed, is purple with lavender bedding, and somehow has even more pillows than Hayden's room. The throw is made with white lace, elegant but not going to keep anyone warm.

'Mum loved lavender,' I say to Aunty Claire. I watch for her reaction. And I am not disappointed when a tear forms in her eyes. She did love Mum, too.

'Yes, we both love lavender. It was a huge part of our childhood – lavender and pearls.'

I leave my bag in the room on an elegant wooden seat, and Aunty Claire shows us the bathroom. She is apologetic that we have to share. We've shared bathrooms our whole lives, although we've never shared a bathroom that's this enormous. I can have a bath while Hayden has a shower. Aside from being huge, it has antiques everywhere. Vases with fresh lavender and even the artwork has pearls around it.

'Don't dillydally,' she says. 'Good night.' She leaves us to it.

It has been a long day, and suddenly, my purple-on-purple giant bed is calling me.

Hayden follows me back to my room. 'What's with the pearls?' he asks.

'No idea, but I remember Mum always wore pearls.

'He heads off to his room, and I'm all alone in the soft comfortable bed. I run my hands between the crisp white sheets. Everything smells of lavender, so I close my eyes. It feels like my mum is with me. I remember she used to wear blue jeans that flared out at the bottom. At nighttime, after dinner, when we would watch TV or a movie, Mum would put on old trackies and embroider flowers on her jeans or jackets. I had them on my clothes and school bags. I wish she had taught me how to make them.

I am jolted back to reality by a crash from below us. The next noise is Hayden running into my room. 'Did you hear that?' he asks. 'New places always have weird noises.' I turn the side light on, and Hayden jumps into my bed, throwing cushions on the floor as he wriggles to find a sleeping spot. I start reading my book out loud. Hayden has fallen asleep before the bottom of the second page. I can still hear shuffling and music. Old music. Almost as if a couple is dancing the waltz but crashing into things as they twirl.

I am too exhausted to read any more, and I follow Hayden to sleep, dreaming about a hill covered in waltzing lavender stems.

Sunday April 10th

B reakfast is cereal and toast, milk and orange juice. All set out on the table with a note saying, *Sorry, I have to work. Come downstairs after 10 o'clock.* I wish she'd joined us – I want to get to know this blood-related stranger better. But at least I don't have to make breakfast – just do the clean up afterwards. As we eat our breakfast in silence, I can't stop thinking that another adult looking after us is leaving us alone; in other words, leaving bloody Hayden in my care. Why does she assume that we can take care of ourselves? Maybe Dad told her.

We do the dishes and make our beds, have showers and get ready for the day. It's 9 o'clock when we finish looking around the flat. So, we stroll outside and explore the town. It's three blocks long. Only three blocks. I don't know the name of the town, but there are large cow statues everywhere. I look across the road, and there is a café with Ed-i-bull hanging over the door on a wooden plaque. As I take in my surroundings, it's obvious all the shops have signs like that. The truck company has Move-a-bull.

'They are bulls, not cows. New Zealand is weird but wonderful,' I say.

'Definitely weird,' Hayden laughs.

An albino cat walks past us on the main road and into a clothes shop. 'Super weird.'

At 10 o'clock, we see the antique shop lights flash on. Aunty Claire walks outside carrying a large French flag. She then pushes a wicker trolley out of the shop. Hayden and I rush over and help her. On the bricks of the shop walls, by the entrance, is a brass plaque, 'Collect-a-bull'. When I step into the shop, I jump, as there is a large chime above me. I look up, and a bell is hanging low, so it rings every time someone opens the door. I'm still studying the bell when Hayden walks in and says, 'What's that smell?'

'Soap,' I say. 'And candles.' The scent is strongly mixed.

'This bowl has soap and walnuts in it. Do you think the walnuts will taste like soap?' Hayden lifts a shell up and sniffs it.

'Best not to try,' I laugh. I see him pocket a walnut – he is more curious than a kitten-that little monkey.

'I have some shop work to do – have a look around, but don't break anything,' Aunty Claire says.

'No guarantees,' Hayden says sheepishly. 'Sorry, but things have a habit of breaking in front of me – it's like I am a magician.' He picks up a top hat that is sitting on a black-and-white striped antique chair and puts it on his head.

'Magicians fix things after they break them,' I say. 'You're more like a clown.'

'Oh, ha, ha,' he says.

'Be careful,' Aunty Claire repeats before she walks away.

My brother is all excited about a Formula One book and a large knife in a box worth over a thousand dollars. I close the case on the knife before he cuts himself.

'Look over there. Have you seen the dog with pearls? Let's play hide and seek?'

'Let's not! And break nothing.'

'I never do – on purpose.'

'I know.'

As we walk from room to room, we see large letters that spells champagne, bowling pins, a brass trumpet player, dog statues.

'She's pretty,' Hayden says, giggling at the naked girl statue.

I pick up a scarf and wrap it around her bodice, giving her some privacy. I swear I see the statue's smile turn upward. When I blink, it's back the way it had been.

'There is a sign by the figs that says 300-years-old.'

'That must be a typo. Maybe the bowl is 300 years old. Either way, stay clear of it.'

'This wine bottle says 1606.' He drops it. I feel my breakfast start coming up as I watch the bottle fall. My breath escapes between my teeth in a rush as the bottle lands on a cushion, not breaking.

'Hold your hands together or get out,' I snarl at him. I pick the wine up and place it safely in the middle of a round wooden table as my heartbeat returns to its normal rhythm.

'I could ride this bike,' he points at an old blue bike with a basket tucked away next to a pile of porcelain plates.

'Or not,' I hiss.

'It looks like it's from the original Wizard of Oz.' Together, we laugh. I can't remember when we've both laughed like this.

'This massive champagne bottle is big enough for the entire cast.'

'Bigger than a munchkin.' We'd watched the movie Wizard of Oz on the plane ride to Wellington. I look at Hayden. He is standing on one leg, flipping the bird at me.

'What are you doing?'

'Being a gnome.'

I see a gnome that is dressed the same as him, jeans and a red and white striped tee. Again, I laugh.

'Your laugh is great,' Hayden says, returning both his feet to the ground.

Once we've walked through the shop's many rooms over five times, spotting new things each time, Aunty Claire calls us to the counter. She spends ten minutes explaining the register and EFTPOS machine to us and then asks me to watch the shop.

Hayden offers to help her. The two of them walk through a back door, and I sit behind the counter.

I sit for thirty minutes before walking around again. I find an old Women's Weekly magazine and read that cover-to-cover and another two magazines before I get a fright from the large chime of the bell over the door. A lady walks in, and I greet her. She looks around for thirty minutes. 'This is all so beautiful,' she says and leaves, buying nothing.

I feel like saying, '*This isn't a museum, you know.*' On average, I have a customer once an hour. They walk in, tell me how beautiful the chandelier or pottery is, look around, and some even take photos, then they leave. No coins spent. How is Aunty Claire feeding herself? Although there are more magazines, I've lost interest in them. The novel I try to read is boring, so I end up playing patience with an old set of cards.

Finally, Aunty Claire and my brother walk in, both red in the face. Aunty Claire asks us to carry the new furniture and pop it inside the shop somewhere. I can't think of anywhere that there is room. But Aunty Claire sits in front of the computer and starts loading photos of the cabinets and chairs on her website. Hayden and I carry the furniture around. We see the naked girl. She's now wearing a crown and feather boa. I swear her grin is more pronounced.

'Did you do that?' Hayden asks me after he places a blue and white toilet down on ceramic tiles.

'No – a customer must have.'

'What's with all the baskets?'

'Some are fruit picking ones, some for flowers, or pastries, or firewood. This one is for grapes,' Aunty Claire says, pointing to an oval one with two portions. I see the price. Almost a thousand dollars.

'Don't break the baskets,' I whisper to Hayden.

We try to squeeze ten pieces of furniture into the room, moving headless mannequins, bookshelves and china stands around. By the time we have finished, the shop is locked up, and Aunty Claire calls us up for dinner.

Together in the kitchen, we make tacos. I cut onion and tomatoes up. Hayden grates and eats the cheese. Aunty Claire questions us all about our lives, school, and hobbies, and she tells us brief stories about her years at school. Mum's name weaves in and out of her stories. Finally, we are getting to know her, to see there is more than just an on-edge stranger. Then she shows us a photo album and tells us about her brother and parents, too. The more she speaks, the more I feel she belongs in our family.

The past connects us. 'Your Mum had more energy than everyone else at school. She would literally climb walls and poles, fences and walls. She was always moving.'

'Like me,' Hayden smiles. 'Dad says I am like the Energiser bunny that just keeps going.'

'You sure are,' I laugh.

'I was always keeping her under control.' Aunty Claire says, looking at me. She understands.

Hayden looks at me too, and laughs.

I am more reckless now,' Aunty Claire tells me.

'So, there is hope for the boring one, then?' Hayden says.

'I am not boring!' I put my hands on my hips.

'You are so! When did you last have fun?'

'I was having fun five minutes ago,' I tell him.

'No – real fun. Uncontrollable laughing.'

'I laugh!' I say.

'Our brother was the sensible one,' Aunty Claire chimes in.

'Where is our Uncle John now?' Hayden asks. 'We haven't met him.'

'We had a fight years ago – your mum and I were obsessed with finding magical treasure, and he said there wasn't any — and it was dangerous.'

'Was there?'

'Not sure if there was a treasure, but it turned out to be too dangerous, and I think that is the reason we lost your mum.'

'So, she didn't leave Dad?'

'No — never. She loved him and you both so much. Something must have happened to make her disappear.'

'Does Dad know?'

'I tried to tell him – he called me crazy and asked me to stay away from you – not give you false hope – oops. Anyway, I won't tell you anymore – I don't want to be told to stay away from you again.'

'Asked to stay away?' I question. Surely Dad hasn't kept her out of our lives.

'Can you tell us more about Uncle John?' Hayden wants more family connection.

'He wanted to live remotely in a country where he could harvest his own food and water and power. I guess he's doing that somewhere.'

'That sounds fun,' I say.

'Sounds lovely to me.' Aunty Clare says. 'But I lost him. I miss them both.'

'I would miss Hayden, so I know what you mean.'

'Oh shucks,' Hayden laughs.

'You two remind me of them so much,' Aunty says. 'Now off to bed.'

It's a magical night, and for the first time, I don't feel like I've been abandoned at a stranger's house. I feel closer to Mum than I have for years. At bedtime, Hayden brushes his teeth and jumps straight into bed with me. 'What's your favourite item downstairs?' he asks.

'I like the mid-century brass duck lamps. How about you?

'He doesn't reply; his breathing's heavier. I drift off, too.

We get a solid six hours sleep before being woken by an almighty thud.

Monday April 11th

We both go to find Aunty Claire, but her bed is empty. 'Aunty Claire, where are you?' I call.

'Why do adults always go missing around us?' Hayden complains.

'She's not missing. She's just somewhere else.' I dash from room to room, calling out as I go.

Hayden follows me slowly. 'She's not here?'

I check every room twice. He's right. 'She's downstairs working.'

'At 3:30 am? Her bed has not even been slept in,' he almost whispers.

I need to find her for me, for her, but mostly for my brother. Still in our PJs, we put on jumpers and shoes and go downstairs to the shop. The shop's back door is open, and we walk in.

'Why does this feel creepy?' Hayden asks.

I shake my head. He's right. All the hairs on my back are standing to attention. The large white letters that spelt Champagne earlier that day are rearranged to say *champ age*. 'Someone's watching us,' I hiss.

'I think they are all watching us. I just saw a statue blink.'

'You did not,' I say, turning towards Hayden.

'He did,' an armless statue laughs.

'Did you hear that?' he asks me.

I want to say no. Statues don't talk.

'Are you ignoring me?'

'I think I've lost my mind.' I say to Hayden.

'I think you have both lost your minds,' another statue says.

'You can hear them, right?' Hayden asks again. I can't admit it. I can't answer yes. So, I say nothing but nod. Help! I'm ready for the looney bin. A clock larger than me is ticking. It hadn't been ticking during the day.

'Aunty Claire, where are you?'

'I hope he hasn't caught her,' a dog statue says in a French accent.

'Who?'

'Can't tell you, I would shatter. Don't want that.'

'You could play charades with us? Then you are not telling us.' Hayden draws a book with his hands.

'No arms.'

I laugh. I can't help it. The tension, missing Aunty Claire, talking statues, it's all too mad! I'm joining the madness train.

'The clock has hands,' a statue says. Both of the clock's hands are pointing to the three – east.

A judge-looking male mannequin with no arms says, 'Get these pearls off me.'

Again I laugh. 'If Harry Styles can wear pearls, you can too.'

'Are you Harry Styles?' Pearlman asks Hayden. We both laugh.

I look at the price-tag, 'These pearls are worth over $6000. You should be honoured to have them around your neck.'

'Please take them off.'

I take them off and look around for somewhere normal to place them. 'Please put them around your neck,' a purple knitted rabbit winks.

'Want a feather boa instead?' Hayden asks from behind a candy floss machine.

'Good grief, no.'

'Please put the pearls on,' a painted lady in a floral hat says from within a golden frame.

'Enough helping,' chimes the grandfather clock. I look up at the ticking clock, and both of his hands are also facing the three.

On the other side, the headless statue is pointing in the same direction as the clocks. I put pearls on my brother and me, and we both head in the direction the helpful furniture is leading us. We end up at one of the new stools we had placed earlier in the day. The embroidered one Aunty Claire got in Foxton.

'Maybe she's treasure hunting?' Hayden says.

'Did you believe all that?' I ask.

'Maybe – then Mum is alive.'

'In that case, I hope she is Mum-hunting.'

'Have some lavender,' a vase full of lavender says as we pass it.

'No thanks,' I reply. It must be a weird dream – I've just spoken to a vase.

'I insist!' The vase spits lavender into our hands. 'Be back by 4 am or you'll get....'

'Enough helping,' the Granddad clock chimes.

'I think we should take the flower,' Hayden says. I feel it's the right thing to do, too. I sit on the stool and somehow slip inside it.

'Jacki....' Hayden's voice disappears.

What happens if I am not back by 4? Why does the furniture have to be so secretive?

The shop is out of sight as I swirl around and around, screaming until my fall slows. Like a flower petal, I twist slowly to the ground, landing gently on my feet. The buildings are all bright colours, vibrant and unique. The trees and shrubs are all sorts of sizes and shapes, as are their leaves and flowers, but they are all shades of grey.

'Hello,' a vibrantly dressed girl with pink hair my age says with a heavy accent. I smile. She walks around a corner. What on earth! She has three legs.

A brown dog, with six feet follows her.

A colourless man is walking my way. He's not wearing bright colours, he's in a black and white suit and black bowler hat. The man from the wardrobe in the back of the van. A tingle goes up and down my spine.

'You must be Janelle's daughter. What a treat. Looking for your mother?' he asks.

I hold up the lavender, and he shivers. He grabs at me. I throw the lavender at him, and he sneezes.

Twisting the pearls around my neck, I say, 'I want to go home.' I fly off the ground slowly and feel a tug on my legs. I kick and reach down. His arms come up, and I swat at them, accidentally undoing his watch. 'Achooooo,' He sneezes again before screaming, 'No!' He's reaching for his watch. I reach too and steal it. Kicking my legs, I swim up in the air out of reach of the bowler man's desperate jumps.

'Come back,' he calls as I float over a magenta building with forest-green windows and a blue roof.

He shoots a gun towards me, but I swoop to my left, and the spray misses me. Why would someone shoot a girl over a watch, and what was the spray made from? I pocket the jewellery and fly away until I'm back in the antique shop, and Hayden is fussing over me.

'You disappeared too. Where did you go?'

'Honestly, I don't know. I think this is all a dream. Let's go back to bed.' I walk out, turning the lights off.

'Did you find any treasure?' Hayden asks. 'Where did you go? Don't ignore me like Dad does!'

He's guilt-tripping me, but I can't tell him. He will get me locked up if I say I have fallen into a world with a three-legged girl and a cartoon-looking man who shot something like cream at me.

'Jackie, did you find the treasure?'

'No, enough about treasure.'

In the morning, I will wake from this nightmare. Aunty Claire will be back with us. Everything will be normal again.

We wake to the sound of the traffic building up outside on the main highway. There's no breakfast laid out for us. No signs of anyone else in here. We look everywhere in the flat, even the linen cupboard, but Aunty Claire hasn't come back to us. We step downstairs. Her van is still parked in the driveway with its engine cold. Hayden and I walk around the town. Even though it's only eight in the morning, the rumbling of cattle trucks never stops. Traffic zooms past us as we walk back to the glamorous flat. She hasn't shown herself by 9:30. The shop is just as I'd left it at 3.30 am.

Hayden says, 'I'm too hungry to go on. If we don't eat soon, I will end up eating one of these bull statues.'

We climb back up the stairs and make ourselves peanut butter on toast. Still chewing, we go down to the shop. As the grandfather clock chimes 10 am, I open the doors. Hayden and I silently sit in the antique shop. No statues talk to us. We don't even talk to each other. The only conversation all day is with the four people that walk in and look around. I see Hayden is looking for something, but he doesn't tell me what. It's when I see him drawing a treasure map of the shop that I assume he's still obsessing about finding treasure.

'The treasure's not real,' I say.

'Maybe Aunty Claire found the treasure, and it was pearls–she has them every-where.'

'Why would she tell us about it if she has already found it?'

One customer almost buys a top hat. He takes lots of photos of him wearing it and says, 'I'll be back before the end of the day.' I send my brother and his map upstairs at closing time, but I wait until 6:20 for the customer. He doesn't return, so I close up shop.

Upstairs, I open the fridge. There isn't a lot in there. Hayden's watching TV — treasure hunters. He has an empty bag of chips and one of my raspberry Foxton Fizzes beside him.

'I'll get you another,' he says.

I want to yell, they don't sell them here, but what was the point? I don't have the energy for a fight. I grab myself a drink while I make dinner. After cracking four eggs, I decide we are having scrambled eggs for dinner. Hayden won't eat mushrooms, so I have to make them twice because I won't eat scrambled eggs without mushrooms. We eat, watching the crazy treasure show and then slip off to bed.

We get a few hours' sleep before banging from downstairs wakes us. I climb down, Hayden at my heels, and the statues jabber at us the minute we walk in.

Tuesday April 12th

'**S**he is still not back. Aren't you gonna save her?' The armless body that the clock calls Xavier says.

'We can't, Xavier! You guys won't tell us what to do.'

'We can't tell you. But your sister knows what to do.'

The Champagne letters today spell *nap game*. I don't know which piece to choose to enter, assuming it must be one of the new furniture pieces, so I cling on to the pearls I've been sleeping in. I walk over to a set of nine drawers. One drawer has a p□ ua shell tied to it. I sit on top of the drawers and feel that sinking feeling. Twisting and turning until I start floating. Saltwater is going up my nose.

I pull my hand up, squeeze my nostrils, and close my mouth. I'm underwater, and

I can't breathe. I don't want to panic, but I'm going to drown. My eyes open, looking everywhere. Seaweed, rocks and me – all under the water, no fish, no houses, no green trees. The only light is from neon flowers on the dark plants. As I look closer at the rocks, I see they have doors, but all the doors are closed.

I want to scream but can't talk under water, so I bend down and pick up some stones. A stone pings as it hits a green stop sign, I hadn't seen before.

It doesn't say stop; it says up.

I throw more stones at the closest doors. Nobody comes out. I feel the air in my lungs dissolve. I quickly grab my pearls and think I want to go home. Instantly, I jerk up again, holding my breath as I rise through the sea water and into the oxygenated air, where I see the brick walls and wooden floor of the antique shop. Big deep breaths, and I jump off the set of decorative drawers, completely dry.

'I want to go with you next time,' Hayden says.

I continue to take big, deep breaths. Even though I can breathe now, I'm still panting. 'Wait, I'm glad you didn't. We could've died down there. I was underwater, and I couldn't breathe,' I tell him and all the statues that were gathered around us about what I have seen. 'No aunty, no mother.'

'And no gold?'

'Forget about the treasure.'

'Which furniture will we explore now?'

'Just me. I need to keep you safe. Maybe we should put stickers on the furniture that we've looked in,' I say. 'I think we should just look at the newly arrived furniture.'

'Yes,' says a mannequin wearing a grey French Army jacket with a red collar.

'Splendid idea,' his comrade mannequin in the black coat with gold buttons in the shape of a V says.

'That is a splendid idea,' Hayden says, trying to copy the French accent. 'You go do that, and I'll wait here.'

I get two different coloured dots – green and red. The red to say we've been there, but it's too dangerous. The green – been there, but it's safe. I walk back and put red dots on both worlds that I've visited. There was something about that scary man that made me not want to go back into the colourful world. His mention of Mum was creepy – everything about him was creepy. And the way he had reached for me, laughing. Is his sneezing the reason lavender is everywhere? Once I put the stickers on, I realise how quiet it has become. The feather in the glass dome with dominoes has stopped humming, and the French dog's tail isn't wagging anymore. Even the rosary beads on the wall that sway like they are in the choir have stopped. 'Where are you, Hayden?' I call out.

The statues all shake their heads.

'I'm so sorry. Did he break one of you?'

Again, they shake their heads and point at a mirror propped up against the couch. I remember the mirror. I'd been scared that Hayden would break it. 'Tell me Hayden didn't go through that mirror, please.'

Nobody says anything as the inventory with heads continue to shake them.

'Was he wearing pearls?'

'Yes,' the dog says in a French accent.

'Lavender?'

'Yes, and you need some.' A vase spits some lavender at me, and I walk up to the Mirror. I slowly fall, and for the second time that night, my world spins round and round. I'm not looking for Aunty or Mum now. My need to find my brother consumes me. When I finally float to the surface, I'm in a grey city. There are large, towering apartments looming over me. But they are all moving mechanically. A robotic dog walks past me. I look around and spy a tree with a bird on it. I can see nuts and bolts on the bird and the branches of the trees – even the leaves. Between branches is a nest that's blowing in the breeze. A robotic man and lady glide past, holding hands, smiling and beeping to each other.

'Excuse me. Have you seen a little boy?'

'Beep, beep, squeak wheeze.'

Well, that was helpful – not!

I spy a vending machine with drinks; suddenly, I'm thirsty, and with a loose coin from my pocket, I put it in the slot and listen to my drink pour. The machine whirls, and out comes a cup. I smell it. Dip my finger in it, cold. It smells really off. It's oil! Everything in this world is a machine, and oil is what fuels them. If my brother is here, he'll be starving.

I run into the middle of the street and scream out. 'Hayden, where are you?' My voice echoes off the buildings and down the street. The buildings seem to move to look at me closer. 'Where are you, Hayden?' I scream again.

There is another stop sign – this time, it's orange and says twist clockwise. Weird. If Hayden is in here, surely he'd come to me. Unless something or someone is holding him back. That bowler hat man? 'Hayden!'

Across the road is an underground train station. An electronic billboard announces a train's arrival. I look closer at the words. 'Hayden was here, but he's gone,' flashes on the screen.

'Where has he gone?' I scream at the screen.

'Another world.'

'Is he safe?'

'He must keep you busy.' '

How can I get to that world?' I ask.

'I can't help.' The words flash up on the screen before it changes to say, 'Next train in five minutes.'

Tightly, I grab my pink pearls and wish myself home.

When I arrive, a teddy bear in a bejewelled tutu asks me what happened. I slide down to the carpet, hoping it won't take me on a carpet ride. Thankfully, I stay still – it's not French. Well, not all of me is frozen. My shoulders shake as I scream and cry. My brother! I attempt to explain to my audience that Hayden was there but is now gone between sobs. They get the general idea.

The TV says, 'That happens. Sometimes, a vortex opens between worlds, but not very often. Only if somebody upsets the residents and they are booted into another world.'

'Unless...' the man in the painted moon says.

'No!' the grandfather clock stops him.

I cry-laugh. Only Hayden could upset a mechanical world so much that they boot him into another dimension.

The grandfather clock ticks, 'Too much information – we are not allowed to help her. You may as well have told her about the jewellery.'

'I assume you won't tell me what that does?'

'Absolutely not – it's with the evil man. No more time tonight. The sun will be rising soon. You need to go to bed.'

'Is the evil man...'

'Bed!' The grandfather's arms are on 3 and 9, almost as if his hands are on his hips.

'Well, how can I possibly sleep while my brother's missing?' I say.

A ceramic vase that looks like it may have once belonged to Hercules spits some more lavender towards me. Lavender won't fix all my problems, but still, I grip the flowers as I turn all the lights off, lock the door and walk the steps up to the lonely flat. I crawl into bed, fully dressed, still gripping the lavender.

Waking up is the only way that I know I've slept. I would have sworn I've tossed and turned awake all night. I have a quick shower, a mandarin and head out the door. I feel like I want to be alone, which is ridiculous because other than talking clocks and teddy bears, I am alone. I head down Main Street, stopping at a café for a hot chocolate. My hands hugging my warm takeaway cup I cross the road just before the bridge. A large helicopter flies close overhead. The noise echoes off all ten buildings on the main road. I walk down and see a path under the bridge. Following along the Rangitikei River, I stroll, taking in the natural ambience until I hear rustling footsteps behind me.

I turn to see a cat. 'Hello there.' I breathe out, excited that it's a real animal, not like the ones I've been seeing in the furniture. As the path threads through a pine forest, the cat follows me. We keep walking a long way till the path opens out on an enormous field. The black and white cat and I cross the grass park. I can see the brick flat above the antique shop. The walk is a loop, so I head towards my Kiwi home and climb the stairs. 'Anyone home?' I call, assuming I'm still alone – but I'm not. I get a reply – a meow. The cat still follows me, and as I make breakfast in the kitchen, the cat lays down by my feet, cleaning itself. Oops, I made too much food. I will save some for lunch. The cat comes to work with me, and I waste hours playing with it and a ball of wool, laser light, and a fluoro orange golf ball. 'I am going to call you Cow. I say patting his black and white fur spots.'

Cow purrs approvingly.

Another quiet, slow sales day in the shop. Back in the flat I feed Cow leftovers, and the two of us curl up on the old-fashioned couch. The soothing purring of the cat lulls me to sleep.

Wednesday
April 13th

It's 3.30 am. 'Bugger it!' I'm up too late, and I've lost so much searching time.

I run down to the shop, holding pearls and lavender, followed closely by my Cow shadow.

'You're late,' the brass gramophone sings in an operatic voice.

'I know.'

'Well, don't dilly dally,' it sings.

Today's Champagne letters spell *man ache*.

I jump into a white ceramic toilet with blue flowers around its base to a silent world. A small kitchen with a table and bench and not much else. I spin around when I see movement in a cupboard.

'Who's there?' A man jumps out of a cupboard and yells, 'Hands up!'

I raise my hands, my pearls gripped tight under my left fingers.

I am about to get out of there when his voice softens, and he whispers, 'Who are you?' There is nowhere to run away from this man. The small room is three meters by three meters, a fridge but nothing else. No bed or carpet or anything. Not even a stop sign.

'Who?'

'Janelle?' He asks.

'Don't hurt me,' I say, stepping away from him.

'I would never hurt you – you look like my sister Janelle. Are you real?' He reaches out and pokes my arm with his unarmed hand, eventually dropping the knife to the ground.

'Uncle John?' I ask. He doesn't look like the pictures of my uncle that Aunty Claire showed us a few nights ago. But he is covered in long scruffy red hair and has a beard which badly needs a trim, so who knows what he really looks like. If only Aunty Claire were still with us. I would sell my left arm to go back to that night we had tacos and hold my family close.

'I'm John.'

'My Uncle John?'

'Yes – any chance you have a spare set of pearls?'

I hand over some pink pearls, and he falls on his knees, laughing like a madman. 'Let's get outta here – nothing good in here at all.'

Together, we grip our pearls and transport. Once back in the antique shop, he looks around. 'Where are we?'

Again, it's eerily quiet in the shop. No laughing cushions, singing gramophones or pointing clocks. The furniture is all frozen. I'm frozen. What if he is not Uncle John and is a madman?

He laughs that scary laugh again. 'Where in the world are we?'

'My Aunt's antique shop.'

'Claire's? Where are my sisters?'

'They are both missing – my brother too!'

'Missing in an antique world?' what I can see of his pale face loses more colour.

'We have to save them.'

'That's what I was trying to do when I found you.'

'Have you seen the black and white man in the bowler hat?'

Eyes in a framed paintings bulge.

Maybe I should have told them about seeing him. 'Yes.' I shiver,

Several pieces of furniture gasp, 'Where?'

'I can't remember. All the worlds are blurring into each other.' He doesn't need to know that I have only actually entered a few. I hope I can trust him, but for now will stay on guard – at least I'm not alone. Thankfully, the furniture doesn't give me away. I wonder if they trust him.

'We need to find and destroy him – this is all his fault.'

'The bowler hat man? How?'

'Barry is a distant relative. Only our blood can enter the Pearl Worlds, but he fell in love with your mum and has tried to capture her our whole lives.'

'Ewww related!'

'Very distantly. Not enough to be creepy – but he is still creepy.

'What I don't understand is how you know Bowler Hat Barry doesn't like lavender. And you entered with a set of pearls. How did both you and Aunty and maybe Mum get caught in the worlds? Why can't you exit with them?'

'That's the golden question. Barry has a spray that dissolves pearls, and he's got a magical item he uses to transfer between worlds with. He's looking for clues but wants to trap all us Pearlers there, so he's the only one with the power.'

'What's a Pearler?' I ask.

'You are. I am. Someone who falls into French antique furniture.'

'And Barry wants to steal our pearls?' I question.

'When he dissolves the pearls, he still doesn't have them, but it means that he controls us. I was living in a world that was in the desert with orange trees. My house was on stilts, surrounded by friendly, yodelling blue chickens. As far as the worlds go, it was a pretty neat place, but he sidestepped into my world, grabbed me and locked me in a room with no joy.'

'Was there a bed? I only saw the kitchen?' I think back to the room I'd found him in.

'There was only the kitchen. I haven't been in a comfortable bed for your entire life.'

'Do you want to sleep now? You can have my brother's bed. 'I want to ask more about the worlds and where my brother and aunty may be. But I have already got lots of information from him and will get more when he's had sleep.

'Sleep in a bed is my dream.'

I turn the lights off in the shop. One world explored today. I only visited one world and found the wrong family member. I hope he can help me find the rest of my family tomorrow morning. He and Cow follow me upstairs.

'Wow! This place is flash,' he says, looking around, probably thinking about what I thought just a few days ago. Each time his head turns to look at a shelf or painting, his long red hair flops over his face. I feel comfortable here now. It's the closest place to my mum and brother, even if I don't know where they are.

'This is mine,' he says, holding up a model aeroplane. 'Oh, that's right, I gave it to Claire for Christmas when we were young. Can't believe she's kept it all this time.' He walks around, picking up books and ornaments, looking in boxes and drawers. Touching each set of pearls he finds on the way. 'Our parents would've been so proud of

Claire and this place,' he mutters. I assume he's talking to himself, so I don't reply.

I show him Hayden's room. Well, the room Hayden's meant to have stayed in. Hayden's backpack with his gear in it is still there, so I move it and store it next to the bag in my room. Hoping Hayden will claim it soon. His bag clatters as I move it, intriguing me to look inside. There are three of my empty Foxton Fizz bottles, little monkey – he can have all of them if he returns home. Hayden belongs here with me, and I'll do anything I can to bring him back. The sun will be rising soon, so there will be no adventures until the next night. No brother nor aunty for another day, no knowing if my mum is lost in a furniture world too.

I drag a set of drawers in front of my closed door. I think he is my uncle – but just in case. I close myself safely in my room for the night.

In the morning, I wake up to another stranger at the dining table. Well, it's Uncle John, but he looks like a man now. Beard and moustache are gone. He smells like lavender, and his hair is short, too. 'I trained as a barber. But still, it is hard to cut my own hair – especially with crafting scissors. 'I don't know what to say, so I say nothing and just smile.

We have breakfast before I show Uncle John around and teach him how to look after the shop. We actually sell an antique plate to a customer. Mrs Anderson collects plates that look like lettuce. She tells me she is a regular and buys a new piece every pay day. She also tells me all about her new grand-daughter and shows me too many photos. And for good measure, she shows me a peach jacket she is knitting for the baby. I hand over the wrapped plate and hope I've not just sold my brother. I take her name and address just in case.

Uncle John quietly watches me process the sale, and then when the doorbell has stopped chiming, he says, 'I have the hang of things; go have some downtime.'

'Are you sure?' I feel bad leaving my Aunt's shop to this stranger, but there is only $100 in the till, and I won't go for long. 'Don't sell Hayden or Aunty Claire!'

I walk around Bulls looking for the local supermarket – needing to stock up on our food supplies. When I can only find a servo,

I head home. I spy on my Uncle John. He is dusting the furniture and talking to it. I leave him for a little longer and head upstairs to make some *Have you lost a cat* posters. It is too quiet in the flat – even with the white noise of the passing traffic and an occasional meow from Cow.

After another spy on the still-dusting Uncle stranger, I head out again to put up my lost cat posters with a sketched picture of my Cow. Cow follows me the whole time.

A group of local kids my age walk up to my poster and laugh.

'Are you laughing at my sketch?' I ask.

'No, not at all.' A girl dressed all in black says – still laughing. 'It's great art – I can see the likeness.'

'All the cats here are strays,' another one says.

'Oh – but he's so friendly.' I pat Cow.

'Well, he's yours if you want him.'

'How do I get cat food for him?'

'Palmy,' one says.

'What?' I didn't understand what he was implying. As if he was telling me to steal it with the palm of my hand. It was not something I planned on doing. I'm no thief.

'Palmerston North. It's the town half an hour that way.' He points to the bridge.

'We go there for everything – it's cheaper.'

'There are a lot of you?' I say, looking between their faces. They are all different ages and ethnicities.

'Our parents work on the base.'

'Base?' I think of things they may mean. Shopping mall? Rocket launch? Softball?

Just then, another large helicopter flies over us, the noise echoing off the buildings.

'That might be Mum home,' a guy says.

'What's the base?' I ask again.

'Ohakea, one of New Zealand's Air Force bases.'

'The best base,' another guy interrupts.

'Yeah,' a chorus of them cheer.

'Air Force base – oh, that makes so much more sense.' I think back to all the aircraft noises I've heard. 'For a small country town, it sure is noisy here.'

'We are the noisiest in Bulls,' a boy around Hayden's age laughs before letting out a scream.

'Let's be loud.'

'Yeah.'

'Let's go.'

'Want to play ruggers with us?' a boy asks me.

'Sure,' I say, not understanding what that means, but I will look dumb asking, so I go with it. I follow them over to a park behind lots of identical two-story brick houses and watch them throw a football around. One girl passes to me, and I catch it, gratefully. I'd paid little attention in PE class.

'What's your name?' A boy comes closer beside me. 'I'm Tama. Here, throw by pulling it back beside you.' He shows me, and I follow his back to the side movement.

Surprisingly, I relax and have loads of fun. 'I'm Jackie.' We throw, catch and tackle each other for an hour until the shortest and youngest calls out, 'Let's play tag.'

We all run around until we are too red-faced to move any more, slumping down under a large tree, puffing and panting. Someone pulls out a bag of lollies and passes them around. They're sour and hurt my tongue, but somehow, I laugh at the tingling. They look at me and laugh, too.

Hayden would love this. Some kids here are his age. I have to find him. My stomach drops. My brother. I can't find him in daylight, and I need him back. I should be sleeping to make the most of my time searching tomorrow morning. 'Sorry, I have to go. This has been great.'

'Let me walk you back,' Tama says. He gets up, and I see a guy wink at him. Is Tama hitting on me? He is sure of himself and cute, but his cheeks blush. His brown eyes look like puppy dog eyes. As we walk, I tell Tama about my Aunty Claire and how I'm staying with her. I don't tell him Aunty Claire is lost inside one of the pieces of furniture. Tama walks into the shop, and I introduce him to Uncle John. Tama stays to help me close up before heading off.

Uncle John and I go to bed straight after tea and wait to be woken by the 'shenanigans downstairs' as Uncle John calls it.

Thursday April 14th

'Where shall we start?' I ask Uncle John as we stumble into the shop in the dark at 3 am.

He turns the night light on. 'Are you sure you can't remember which world you saw Bowler Hat Barry in?'

I walk back, looking at the furniture that I've dotted with stickers. Walking past the white letters, *peach nag.*'

My first world – grey scale trees, bright colours everywhere else. The man was black and white like the plants. 'It was this one,' I point at the stool from Foxton. 'I remember I found him the first trip.'

'You'll need lavender,' the ancient vase says, spitting the purple flower at us. We hold our pearls, put the flowers in our pockets and jump into the Pearl World, whirling.

We land in the same place. This time, I understand travelling and the worlds better. We look left and right, searching, for the bowler hat man. No sign of him □ just the purple road and pink pavement; yellow, orange, and green buildings; and some grey tulips.

'What now? Where should we head?' I ask Uncle John. We hadn't even made a plan if he was there. This time, I note a stop sign I had missed last visit. Green with '□' on it. I swear I see John look at it. 'What are the signs?'

'Not sure.' His body stiffens up. He knows alright. I want to find out, but not as much as I want to find my family.

'Drop these pearls by mistake,' Uncle John tells me.

'I can't see her in here. Let's go,' he says loudly.

Uncertain, I drop the spare pearls – and we fly till we are slowly spinning and plop back in the Bulls antiques shop. My head is foggy, gutted to have returned from another world without my brother.

'Stand over there.' Uncle John points to an area around the corner. He heads into another room and comes back with a large fishing net from a corner cabinet. 'Who was the local boy from earlier?' the armless lawyer statue asks.

'He was cute,' the gardener in the floral painting says.

'I saw the way he looked at you,' the knee-high brown leather boots with wooden stands in them adds.

'Mmmmhmmm,' plays the trombone.

'He likes you,' teases a bronze tin jug.

My checks blush pink.

'Focus!' Uncle John hisses.

'Thanks,' I whisper. They all heard me.

Just then, Bowler Hat Barry appears. Pearls in his fingers. 'Ehhh that smell.' He screws up his face. So, he's the reason lavender is everywhere. He hates the over-powering smell of lavender in the shop. 'Ah-hhchoo.' The man recovers from sneezing and wheezes. 'John, she's Janelle's little girl – like her, only black.'

'Don't be racist,' the French dog huffs.

'Give me my watch,' he screams, lunging at me.

Uncle John does it so quickly – I don't even realise what's happening, he reaches out, nets the man, and pushes Barry into the decorative toilet. Leaving only the bowler hat off balance, twirling on the wooden floor. Then, before I have a chance to ask, 'What's going on...' Uncle John jumps in the toilet. Ten seconds later, he spins back out and kicks the chamber pot. It makes a scream, and I do too. Uncle John falls down, panting on the floor, while the pot lies in two different pieces. He shakes and shakes, and I sit on the chair, pearl-less, consoling him like I used to with Hayden.

'That man has tormented me my whole life, and now I can finally live.'

'Did you kill him?'

'No – he's stuck in there forever.'

'What if Mum, Hayden or Aunty Claire are in that world?' my body rocks forward and back.'

They aren't,' he tries to assure me – unsuccessfully – 'I checked.'

'How do you know? You were only there for a second!' I shake too.

'Promise – I know that world. There is nothing but that one room. Nowhere else at all. I had no one's company for years. It was horrible.'

'Oh,' I say, understanding I hadn't lost anyone else. But what if I couldn't trust John? Is he really my uncle? I don't like Bowler Hat Barry, the way his smile crept higher on one side of his mouth, but I don't know the man claiming to be my uncle either. I'm still consoling him. Barry did call him John. Do I trust Barry, though? No!

'Do you have his watch?' he asks.

'The first time I met him, he snatched me, I grabbed at him, and his watch came off. Then I threw lavender at him and escaped with his watch while he sneezed. It's upstairs somewhere.'

'That watch is magic – show me later, but for now, we have time for another world. Which furniture have you not looked in?'

Finally, we could enter more than one world per morning. 'These ones,' I point to the pile I've made of the new unsearched items. A small, embroidered footstool jumps up and down and says, 'Pick me!'

'No helping,' booms the grandfather clock. His head nodding all the same. I pick up the bowler hat and hang it on a coat rack.

'Don't put that disgusting thing on me,' the rack says, shaking it to the ground again.

I look around, and all the furniture's shaking their bodies to me. I put the hat on the floor in the corner of the room behind a yellow floral chair. Puffy-faced Uncle John and I hold on to our pearls, plus an extra set, and fall into a world of blue trees and translucent leaves via a puffy cream chair with loose threads that feel like it's giving me a hug.

'Hayden!' I call out.

Uncle John stares at me. 'Shhh!'

'Haven't you just got rid of our enemy? We're safe now, right?' For now, this stranger is all I have, so I will have to trust him – but I will have another look at the photos and make sure he is my long-lost Uncle John.

'Our human enemy is gone. I don't know this world □ for all I know, it may have green man-eating bears,' he warns.

'How about large scary fluffy pink monsters?' I quiver, pointing at one. The world smells like candy floss – surely, they're not candy floss monsters.

We climb a blue-barked tree each and hide while the strangest fluffy beast storms past us, grunting. Once it's gone, we slide down again.

'Over here,' a woman's voice beckons. We run towards the voice, and both charge into Aunty Claire's arms.

'Barry stole my pearls, and Janelle's not here.'

'So good to see you,' Uncle John says.

'There's another sign,' I point to the stop sign with a red downwards arrow on it, out to Uncle John.'

'It's nothing,' he lies.

'Talk later □ there are hundreds of monsters, and they are all hungry. Let's go!' We hear more roaring stomping our way. I hand over a set of pearls, and the three of us twirl away to reality again.

Aunty Claire speaks first. 'John, is it really you? Where have you been? Africa?'

'No, inside a toilet pan.'

'For how long?'

'Fifteen years?'

'I am so sorry. We had the fight, and I thought you disowned us. I tried so hard to find you when Janelle went missing.'

'I found a piece of the clue.'

'You believe?'

'Yes, I believe.'

Aunty's stomach grumbles just as Uncle John is about to tell us about his clue. 'Come, let's go upstairs. I'm starving. We can talk more up there.'

We follow her out, but not fast enough. She turns off the lights as she exits her shop, leaving us scrambling in the dark, trying not to break anything. I want to ask if we can search for Hayden in other worlds, but the two adults are lost in adult chat and ignore me.

'So glad to see this place again,' Aunty Claire says, walking through her boring front door into the lavish world inside. She looks at my cat sideways.

'I named him Cow 'cause he's black and white, and there are so many bulls in this town, I thought it needed more cows.'

She laughs and pats him. 'He's friendly – maybe he's someone's pet.'

'I have lost cat posters up in the streets.'

'Well done. Looks like you have it covered. I'm exhausted. Is Hayden asleep?' She asks.

I look down at the ground. How do I tell her? Maybe the tears rolling down my cheek will be enough to let her guess.

Uncle John replies for me. 'He's lost. He went looking for you and the treasure, alone – and hasn't returned...'

'I'm sorry – I should never have said anything about the treasure. I was scared you would look for it. We'll find him tomorrow or soon – I promise.'

'But you haven't found Mum in years of looking,' I say.

'Thats because I don't know what she went missing into. Hayden is downstairs – we'll look in everything until we find him.'

'Promise?'

'Promise!' they both say.

She embraces me. I wonder what she's been through with the pink fluffy monsters. She feels weaker than she used to. 'What happened to you in there?'

'He dissolved my pearls.'

'He, being Barry?' I flop on the chair opposite my aunty and uncle, 'Yeah, he has a gun with a solvent that dissolves pearls. Without them, we can't return.'

'Does it look like clear?'

'Yes. Did you see him?'

I nod. 'Is that why you always take a second set?'

'That and so I can give a string to Janelle when I find her.'

'Did you have two sets in that world?'

'Yeah, I ran away and used the second pair. When I thought I was safe, he appeared again.'

I walk into the kitchen and heat some leftovers while Uncle John tells me how he was trapped. Using the how to make a pavlova tea towel, I take the hot plate of shepherd's pie to Aunty Claire.

'Thanks love.'

'Can I please see the watch?' Uncle John asks.

'Wait – she has the watch!'

'Potentially, Barry thinks she does.'

I walk into my room and bring the old gold watch back out.

Aunty Claire looks at it and jumps up from her gold-trimmed chaise, running downstairs. Uncle John and I follow. 'Wait!' he calls after his sister.

We grab a set of pearls plus a spare one each. I put my spare string in a plastic bag and jump into a new world. Before I have a chance to look around at the neon city with neon elephants, Aunty Claire turns a nob on the watch with a click. I want to see more of that glowing world. It has a stop sign, but I don't see what it said. We blur into a pastel forest world that smells like Christmas. But all I see is a blur of apricot, buttercup and lilac pine trees. And with a turn, we change again, thousands of singing parrots in every possible colour. Each turn, we change places. No mum, no brother, no time to look around. Then she unwinds, and we go back to the second pastel world, the first neon world, and fall back to Bulls, where the only bird I can hear is a ruru singing, 'more pork.'

Back in the magical shop in front of the ferns with fairy lights shimmering away, Aunty Claire lies on the black-and-white checkered tiles, giggling. Uncle John and I can't help but join in.

'We can find Janelle now. I don't have to own the furniture to enter the worlds – I can sidestep into them. Thank you.' She hugs me, giving me lots of small kisses on my forehead.

'Just remember Barry is in one of them,' Uncle John says.

'And he's tricky,' I add.

'My brother transferred worlds – he started in one but wasn't there when I went in to find him. The world told me he had left but not to the shop – he crossed over somehow – did Barry move him?'

'Possibly. Bugger, maybe I shouldn't have trapped Barry. Sorry, I didn't question him – I was angry and acted irrationally.'

I open a cupboard and bring out the pieces of the toilet pan – the world Barry's trapped inside.

'We can repair this if we don't find my sister and your brother soon. But only if we have to – I don't want us getting trapped in there. I never want to see that room again,' Uncle John shivers.

'Bedtime,' Aunty Claire says as the grandfather clock chimes, then goes silent. All the eyes blink into the background, or grains of wood, or scratches in the paint. I wipe my slimy over kissed forehead. This time, Uncle John and I leave first to avoid the dark obstacle course.

Cow and I head straight to bed while Uncle John and Aunty Claire catch up. Now and then, I overhear words like, 'Poor Janelle,' 'You got him,' and 'Oh, I have missed you.' At least I now know he is my Uncle John – I do have support. They will help me find Hayden... and Mum.

We drive to Palmerston North early the next morning for food and cat supplies. Aunty Claire and Uncle John have the shopping under control, so I'm allowed to wander around the mall looking in all the closed shop windows. The shops open as we leave to drive back to Bulls.

We are back in the antique shop just in time for 10 am. As there are no customers, I show them my sticker system on the new furniture and explain the worlds I've visited to them. Aunty Claire has a system too, and she combines my information with hers. She tells me to go for a walk, so Cow and I head to the park from yesterday. The same guys are there and call me over. We play bull rush, and then one mum calls everyone to her house for lunch. Tama insists I follow, and we eat bacon and egg pie with raspberry Raro which is like our Cottees. I love it. We stay at that kid's house and watch a movie, then at the shop's closing time, Tama walks me home again.

We have lamb roast for dinner, with mint sauce and herbed gravy that Aunty Claire has been cooking all day. 'This tastes like the roasts Mum used to make,' I say. 'Last I knew, your mother was a vegetarian.'

'Oh no – your Dad is meat obsessed,' Uncle John says.

'It was just a Janelle phase,' Aunty Claire says. It sounds like they used to say lots of things were Janelle phases. 'How is your father? He was my best friend. That's how your parents met,' Uncle John adds.

'Yeah, but you never liked them together,' Aunty Claire butts in.

'Only because she changed who she was for him.'

'She changed for whomever she was around – not just him. Plus, she also changed around you and was so depressed when she thought you'd disowned us. Janelle always looked up to you.'

'I suppose you're right.'

I want to find her – and my brother. 'I am going to sleep now,' I say, leaving the dishes for once.

Cow and I are in bed by 7.30.

Friday April 15th

U ncle John wakes me at 2:45 am. I love how he treats me like a child. He hands me a decorative silver tray. On it is toast with a thin spread of marmite, a banana, and a hot chocolate. He's protective, and I don't have to be on guard all the time around him now.

It's even rubbing off on Aunty Claire, too. She sits on my bed and tells me a story about my mum breaking her arm playing football. I can't imagine my mum running around with a ball – but I have to admit I'm laughing, trying to imagine it.

Aunty Claire decides that we will separate for this morning's search. I have to stay in the shop while she and Uncle John each Hayden-hunt in different worlds. 'If we are not out in 30 minutes, come get us.' I want to be treated like a child more, but not like this. I need to find my brother. I pace around the shop, see the large white letters *each pan*. One more morning here – I wonder what the words will spell tomorrow. How many word combinations can they make out of the word Champagne?

The jar of spoons and I play Who am I? but they are not very good at it. They don't even know what animal, mineral, and vegetable are! We try to play truth or dare, but that fizzles out too. I then kill time by sketching flowers on a blackboard that laughs every time I erase my drawings. Aunty and Uncle each search six worlds in thirty minutes. Between each world popping out to give me negative progress reports.

Uncle John comes out, holding a bloody arm, red-faced, and trying not to wince.

'What happened?' I wrap a nearby tea towel around his arm.

'A rainbow-coloured momma hippo. They are vicious when they're agitated.'

I don't know whether to laugh or cry. Imagine being bitten by that! I take away his pearls and settle him in a chair. If I leave the pearls on him, who knows where he might end up? I have seen no worlds that are commercial – nothing like a hospital to go to when hurt, or a restaurant if hungry. How cool would it be if we could fall into KFC for a 3 am snack! What is wrong with me? Uncle John is bleeding, and I am thinking like Hayden.

'Claire,' he stammers.

I put on pearls and fall into the painting I last saw Aunty Claire enter. She's in a world that is all chalk drawings – ironic. I lean against a house, and it rubs a little out – oops. The stop sign in this world is red chalk and says 'up'.

'Hey,' an apple-green chalk man calls from a window. 'You've locked me inside. The last of your kind that came this way locked me in the house for a week. Draw back my front door, now!'

'Sorry.' I find some chalk and draw a handle with a large lilac rectangle around it.

'What street number are you?' I call up to him.

'One hundred and three.'

'Aunty Claire!' I call out loud as I chalk the numbers on the door. I can't help it. I start drawing a flower garden on the side of the chalk man's house.

Opening his newly drawn door, he comes to stand beside me. 'That's great. Can you give my bedroom a makeover?'

I laugh and pick up a pink chalk to create some roses. I swear I can smell the sweet blooms. Should I draw a lemon tree? I decide I will and a larger orange tree beside it.

'Thanks, you are nicer than that other human.'

'Sorry – was it a lady with strawberry blonde hair?'

'No, a man with a bowler hat.'

'You don't have to worry about him □ we locked him away a few nights ago.' Thinking of Barry, I draw lavender with a purple scribble, inhaling the safe smell it now gives me.

'I saw him earlier today. Thankfully he wasn't here long enough to do damage this time.'

'No!' I gasp.

'Jackie,' Aunty runs towards me. 'Why are you here? You were meant to wait. Are you okay?'

She embraces me, and I leave white chalk handprints on the back of her black denim jacket.

'Uncle John is hurt.' I decide not to tell her about Barry being on the loose again.

Together, we return to the shop. 'We can't leave you,' Aunty Claire says.

'We will look after her,' the grandfather clock chimes.

'Take him quick,' the British dog says.

Reluctantly, Aunty Claire drives Uncle John off to an accident and emergency centre out of town.

Back to treating me like an adult. Talk about hot and cold! I guess I said they could leave me, but they don't know Barry is free again.

I look in the spot where I'd hidden Barry's hat and it's gone. 'Where's the hat?' I ask the furniture. They all turn away from me and the grandfather clock has the nerve to whistle. Are they on my side or what? Not wanting to spend any more time with them, I decide to try the last two worlds that Aunty Claire planned to visit that night. I take two sets of pearls, tuck one under my shirt and grip onto the other.

'Don't – I am in charge.' The clock says. But he also points to the decorative side drawers. I open a drawer and jump in.

Inside the drawers are cats playing board games. 'Come play,' speaks a tabby cat in a British accent. I don't want to anger the cats in case they turn into lions or tigers – and I hope they are not cheaters. I roll the dice. 'Six.' I move a giant blue token forward six spaces and then up a ladder. As the ginger cat takes his turn, I look around. No brother. No mum and not a stop sign in sight. But what a fun place to visit. I wish I could come back with Hayden, Tama and the others, and we could have a wonderful time winning and losing. I watch a black and white cat win a game of Connect Four before it breaks into a cat dance. Something about this place makes me think of all the stray cats in Bulls. Have they come out of a world like this? Should I bring them in here to give them a better life? I throw the purple and orange dice again and roll a three. No snakes or ladders on this turn. I could easily get lost in here, but my brother isn't here, so I step back and grip my pearls. I want to go home. Spinning, I step onto the red carpet surrounded by antiques.

'Still no luck?' A king embroidered on a cushion asks.

'Don't give up, love,' the matching embroidered queen says. I love the embroidered cushions – they remind me of Mum, needling pictures when I was young. I miss her so much. Clutching the pearls tight, I fall into the last world on the list. My eyes are blinded. I blink as I focus on the yellow. Everything is yellow. The sky, the grass, the trees, just all different shades of yellow. Mustard, canary, corn and brass. Rotten lemon smells twist my nose – I hold my breath to stop the gagging sensation.

'Thank goodness,' Hayden screams, running towards me. 'There are yellow dinosaurs in here, the man-eating type!'

Before he can reach me, a dinosaur charges between us. I can't get the pearls to him. I can leave the world. Come back for him. What will he think if I go?

'Hey, want a steak dinner?' I call the prehistoric beast's attention my way while Hayden climbs a tree. As the yellow-horned freak charges at me, I grip my pearls, fly up home.

'What happened?' the spoons chant. But I don't reply. I fall back into the lemon world. Swimming in the air till I'm above Hayden's tree. He reaches up for the spare pearls, and we both leave that world, hoping to never return. I smile, kiss his forehead, hand him pearls, and we twirl back to safety.

The furniture cheers when they see Hayden. I hold him tight, smelling his sour lemon hair. My brother! I found him. The furniture that has hands or legs clap them as they see Hayden. Hayden, ever the showman, takes a bow, and I laugh. Such relief to have him home again.

'No more treasure hunting. I'm not losing you again! You got that?'

'Sure.' He winks at the horse painting, and it winks in return. He turns to face me and laughs, wrapping his arms around me again. 'Oh, you sook – did you miss me?'

'Not at all,' I sob as the furniture tells him the truth. 'Shh, you lot, and good night.' I turn off the shop lights and lock the door soundly. I don't want anyone getting in – but more importantly, I don't want Barry getting out.

'We need to find Aunty Claire,' he says as we walk upstairs. 'It's horrible being stuck inside there. I wouldn't wish that on my worst enemy.'

'I have her and Uncle John.'

'Where?' He yells, running up the steps two at a time and looking all around the flat.

'They will be back soon.' I make him have a shower to get rid of the rotten citrus smell that's lingering and get him up to date while he washes between his toes and behind his ears. Hayden falls asleep in my bed as soon as he's dried and dressed, and we sleep until the sun rises.

We both jolt awake as Aunty Claire screams, 'Hayden!' He sits up, rubbing his eyes, and is scooped in a hug.

Uncle John enters my room and introduces himself. We have a rushed breakfast before Aunty Claire and I open the shop while the males get to know each other.

Aunty Claire categorises the world Hayden's been lost in and the other ones we visited last night. We have time while the sun's up to plan tonight's visits, but then we sleep. My eyelids are so heavy I'm looking forward to the large lavender bed.

'Only Mum left to find,' I say to Aunty Claire as she moves the yellow world Hayden was lost in and hangs the mirror on an empty hook.

'We have searched these – they are all for sale now. I need to move them so I can afford new ones to search.'

'You can just use the world changer?'

'John and I have been talking about that and about Barry.'

'Um, about Barry.' I swallow. 'The chalk man said Barry was in the chalk world yesterday morning □ is time different in there than here?'

'No – shit!'

'Aunty Claire!' I've never heard her swear, but I guess it is an S kind of moment.

'Sorry, love, I thought we were finally safe.' I help her open the shop as we chat.

'Maybe he has another world changer.' 'He is good at tinkering and making things. Bugger.'

'We go home tomorrow. What if he follows us there?'

'You have pearls. I will give you back the watch, and you have an adult with phones you can call anytime, day or night.' She places the watch on my wrist.

'But you can use this to find Mum?' I say.

'Your Mum would rather you were safe.' I look down at it, four tiny pearls embedded in each corner. The watch is dainty and looks too feminine for Barry or Uncle John. It suits me perfectly.

'I am sorry I wasn't here for your entire stay. Will you come back again? I hardly got to know you.'

'I would love to next holidays.'

Tama walks into the shop.

'Hi Tama, this is my niece,' Aunty Claire smiles.

'Yes, we've met,' he says, blushing.

'I think he likes you,' my Aunty Claire says far too loudly. It makes both Tama and I turn redder than the red on the French flag we're standing in front of.

'What's going on here?' Hayden and Uncle John stumble through the back door.

'Hi, I'm Tama, you must be Hayden. Your sister talks so much about you. My sister never talks like that 'bout me.'

'Who, her?' Hayden says, pointing at me and laughing.

'My brother's your age – want to come play bullrush?'

'Sure,' Hayden grins, 'see you.'

'Jackie's coming too – she's a laugh a minute.'

'Who? My sister? She plays sports and laughs?'

'Ha ha,' I joke as I steal Hayden's Rabbitoh's cap and run off down the road with it.

'Who's that girl, and what did you do with my sister?' Hayden calls as the two of them run after me, only catching up as I wait to cross the main road.

We join the other kids, but Hayden sits still □ which is new for him. He watches me throw the ball around like a Wallaby – or All Black – till finally he joins in. We have a ball, as we chase it around the field in clusters. Rain clouds burst open, but we keep playing. We go into mudslides until the sky lights up like fireworks, and everyone calls out, 'catch ya later.' We're halfway home before the thunder rumbles each side of the main road. The sky glows again as three planes fly overhead. There must be a no rugby in electrical storms rule that everyone obeys.

Back at the flat, I put our muddy clothes on to wash while Hayden has a shower, and then he and Uncle John head off for a drive. I read an old book, which I'd found in a cupboard downstairs, surrounded by bubbles in the bath. It's relaxing. I'm sad that we have to go home tomorrow. I'll miss this enormous bath and all the lavender soaps, and the smell of bacon hock soup boiling away that I haven't had to make but get to eat, plus being covered in mud with Tama. I will miss Tama. Even the New Zealand accent – I used to think it was annoying, but it's grown on me, and it's kinda cute now – especially the way Tama talks.

After another early meal, we do the dishes, and I sink into the lavender pillows. I can't sleep. My chat with Aunty Claire rolls around in my head. Was she asking me to search at home for Mum? Is that why she gave me back the watch? It's my last night here to find Mum. I will try antique shops back home. I will look everywhere. Aunty Claire told me she may not be missing in an antique shop. She may be inside someone's house. No one knows where she is – but I have to look everywhere. Because we have an early morning flight, we are told to sleep all through the night instead of getting up and doing a 3 am search but I want Mum home.

I want to be a child again.

Saturday April 16th

Still tossing and turning, I recklessly sneak downstairs alone at 3 am with two sets of pearls. First, I head to the white letters; the 'M' is upside down, and it spells *WE CAN* 'We can find Mum!' I say to the furniture. They give me words of encouragement. One set of pearls for me and one for Mum. I plan to slip into every item in the first room, calling Mum's name, waiting thirty seconds, then, trying the next one. Aunty Claire told me she'd checked them all – but what if she'd made a mistake? What if Barry moved her from one world into another, and she is here somewhere? I start with a cane wicker basket filled with picnic plates and cups.

Stepping into the chair I can smell relaxation before the world comes in to view. I land between a row of lavender. Plains of the scented flower are everywhere. I look until they meet rolling hills where there are large spheres, I run towards the shining rocks and realise they are giant pearls. And away from the lavender, the pearls smell of sea salt. The weather is perfect, with blue sky and a few fluffy clouds to make shapes with. Of all the worlds, this world makes me want to stay in here forever. This relaxing paradise has no stop sign. I skip around looking and breathing. I wish I could hang out in here to read, paint and even do pilates like Mum used to do – Mum! That's why I'm here. I look at my watch and see I only have 35 minutes left to find Mum. I hold my pearls and say I want to go home as I float up. I take one last look at the amazing lavender and pearl world, maybe one-day I can revisit this one.

Feet on the cold, musty and dusty chess-board floor I walk towards an elegant walnut table and its six chairs. The first chair I go in – nothing but a horse stable with pigs wearing saddles. Inside the second chair is a table and chairs the same as the seat I've just fallen into. Only the long oak table is set with the most amazing Christmas dinner.

Red, green, and gold decor and crackers. At the end of the table, I see a sleeping human-sized Christmas fairy with long fine white hair. She is so magical I feel drawn to stare at her, but I realise there is something familiar about her. 'Mum?'

She flutters open her blue eyes and looks at me. 'Jellybean?' she says.

'Mum,' I scream as I run to her. She covers her mouth with her index finger and signals for me to hide under the table. I dart under just in time.

Vibrating steps shake the world as large hairy feet walk past. 'Did you say something Angel?'

'I fell asleep and was sleep talking, dreaming of my Mum.'

'Enough talking about you. Back to me,' the voice booms.

I scurry over on my hands and knees to Mum and hug her legs, silencing my sobs. I reach into my pocket as the giant hairy-legged thing starts to talk about his news. 'What will we eat for dessert?'

Quietly, I slide the extra string of pearls into Mum's hands. Mum grips them tight with her left hand, and with her right, she holds up three fingers, then two, and finally one.

A second later, we are both flying and spinning above the table and the ugly-looking troll.

The giant below us at the table screams, 'Come back, Christmas Fairy. I will be a good boy. The hat man said you were my gift. Come back.'

Once our feet are on solid ground at the antique shop, surrounded by many turn-of-the-century black top hats, Mum and I connect in the best embrace of my life.

We hear Hayden say from around the corner, 'I can't lose my sister, help me find her, please.'

'We will search every world and in each piece of furniture looking for her,' Aunty Claire assures him. 'Glad she wasn't wearing the watch, or we'd have no hope.'

'You don't have to look for me. I'm here – and I found someone.'

'Here they are,' a horse's head announces us.

'Hayden?' Mum sobs, clinging onto me. 'Oh, you are so big,' Mum reaches out.

Her brother and sister join our embrace, but Hayden doesn't move.

'Is she really our Mum?' Hayden asks.

'She is,' I confirm.

'Is your Dad here?' Mum looks around, hopeful.

'He's working,' Hayden complains.

'Oh Hayden, you look so much like him.' Mum turns to her sister. 'I hope I haven't lost him.'

'He's still single – but he's not the same,' Aunty Claire replies.

'Mum?' Hayden says again. His face is so puffy. I want to help him. Mum walks over to him. He moulds into her, letting out a sobbing noise I've never heard him make before. I take a step towards them, then freeze. This is their moment, and it's Mum's turn to mother him. What will my job be, now? Just a sister? I'm not sure I even know how to do that.

Aunty Claire slides beside me and holds me close to her. She understands what it's like to be an older sister. I find myself crying in her arms till the five of us connect again.

All letting out the emotions we have held onto for so long.

After five minutes, my eyes are swollen, and my heart is healing. I can't cry anymore, and somewhere from deep inside my stomach, a giggle bubbles to the surface. I have my mum, and an aunty and uncle. My brother's perfectly chaotic, and Dad will get his wife back. I'm overjoyed – not sad anymore.

My giggling spreads like Hayden's tears until we are all laughing. We close the shop and head upstairs.

Aunty quickly shows Mum around, and the three siblings talk about their past and future while Hayden and I fall asleep with Cow purring between us.

When we wake, which seems like only a minute later, everyone's in a panic. 'Hurry, boarding is in two hours,' Aunty Claire bellows.

'How long to get there?' It had taken us a whole day to drive here with all the stops along the way. I remember that was the first time I had seen Barry. He'd been in the van with us.

'Two hours.'

Sheesh. I don't even get to say goodbye to Tama and the others. I hope they will understand. I give Cow a squeeze and a chin tickle.

Hayden and I are still packing our bags as we load into the French antique shop van and head to Wellington. Over the bridge and past the Air Force base. No time to stop at Foxton and top up my fizz supplies.

Mum and her siblings talk the entire trip catching up on years of politics, global warming and world economics.

'Has anyone told Dad?' I interrupt them as we clamber out of the van and head inside the airport.

'I meant to - it crossed my mind at 4 am but I didn't know what to say,' Uncle John says.

'I guess I will be his surprise – I can't wait to see him.' Mum almost sings.

Dad's pacing looking at his watch as we charge to the departure gates at the Wellington airport – Hayden's and my bags finally squeezed closed. We only have a carry-on bag each. Dad's head jerks up, no doubt as he hears us. Mum runs up to him, her arms wide to finally hold him again. Dad goes stiff and backs away.

'Oh James. Look how big they are - thank you for looking after my babies,' Mum cries, stepping back towards him and grasping his shirt.

'Let go of me,' he says, stepping back again. 'Where have you been! Why didn't you reach out to us, to them.' He steps away from Mum and pulls Hayden and I in under his arms. 'They are my kids – you can't come back into our lives after abandoning us all for eight years and want to take them from me.'

'Honey,' Mum stammers, 'I love you.'

'You left us – without so much as a word.' Dad is using his grumpy voice, but tears have given him away as they dribble out the corner of his eyes.

'I was kidnapped – I would never leave you and the kids by choice. And Jellybean saved me.'

'It's true, we have been saved and re-turned here,' Uncle John says, stepping to-wards his best friend.

Dad looks at them both like they have COVID and shakes his head.

'Final call for passengers to Sydney Australia,' crackles all over the airport.

'Come on, Mum,' Hayden says, pulling her towards us. 'I don't have a passport – can't travel.' Mum has been too busy catching up to realise she couldn't travel with us. We will be separated again.

'I have a plan,' Aunty Claire says. 'You won't like it – but it will get you home.' The two of them walk off to the toilets, and Aunty Claire comes back with a jewellery box. 'Take care of this – your mother's in here.'

'What's she talking about?' Dad shakes his head. 'Has she disappeared again?'

In hushed tones on the plane, I tell Dad all about the secret Pearl Worlds, the man with the hat, Mum, Uncle John, and Tama and the Air Force kids.

The whole time I grip onto Mum's box - the most precious item I've ever held.

In my story telling I leave out the hungry yellow dinosaurs and candy floss monsters. I don't know if he can handle everything in one go. 'My favourite world was inside a picnic basket - amazing fields of lavender.' I say.

'That sounds relaxing.' He replies as If he really does believe me.'

I wish I had asked Aunty If I could buy the picnic basket.' I also tell him all about my new friends, especially Tama. And my newfound love for rugby.

'Isn't tennis safer? Less broken bones?' Dad asks.

I laugh it off and he looks at Hayden.

'What!' I ask my eyebrow creasing. 'You laugh like your brother. Sounds like you act a little more like him too now.'

'I am not hypo - but yeah - I love running around and laughing. Man, I wish I'd grabbed more Foxton Fizz.' I keep telling him about our trip as Hayden sleeps on Dad's shoulder the whole three hours. Hayden talks all through customs - his stories are more about his time alone lost.

'You lost your brother?' Dad's eyes bulge at me.

'I found my brother.' I ruffle Hayden's hair and he gives me a snuggle.

Once in Sydney Hayden talks the whole car trip home until we arrive at our front door. I can't wait to get Mum, so as soon as we put our bags down in the lounge, I put on my pearls. I give Dad and Hayden a set each and hold on to Dad. They follow me into the musical box.

'I am going to be sick,' Dad says as we stop spinning.

We're in an opera with ballet dancers everywhere. The only person not spinning is Mum. As beautiful as ever, Mum dances over to us, and together, we sway. Dad embraces her. Really holds her close, smiling as she whispers in his ear. He listens while she explains her story. As she talks, his head shakes less. By the end of her story, Dad's arm has draped around her neck, and Mum leans in towards him. We grip our pearls and leave the magical box, I have a feeling we will use that again. I think they need some privacy, so I pull Hayden with me first to unpack and then make lunch. We carry four plates with sandwiches into the lounge and interrupt our parents' kissing.

Hayden makes a face at me, and I laugh.

Mum and Dad pull apart.

'Oh love, you shouldn't have to make meals,' Mum says. Dad apologises. He explains how I stepped up to help him and

shows Mum all our achievements and photos. At dinner time, Mum and Dad cook together. Hayden and I stay close, listening to
each of their stories and adding our own.
After dinner, Dad brings out Mum's embroidery kit. 'Mum, I love how you used to do
this when I was a child. Can you please
teach me? She smiles at me, 'Absolutely, it
would be a dream come true.'

Dad unwraps his arms from around Mum
and stands. 'While you guys get lost in your
embroidery, I'm gonna go and fluff around
in the kitchen. Does anybody want a raspberry drink?'

'Absolutely!' Mum and I reply grinning as
we sew lavender on a pair of my jeans. 'Hayden, do you want to know how to embroider
a dinosaur?'

'Shit, no!' he says. I laugh as Hayden is
told off for swearing.

I guess Mum and Dad kiss more as Hayden
and I do the dishes.

Alone in my room, I write a farewell letter
to Tama, I really want to stay friends with
him – he taught me to be free and laugh
again. Envelope sealed, teeth brushed,

emotionally shattered, I fall asleep, leaving our parents to be adults.

Sunday April 17th

Sunday is calm.

We have family time together in the lounge once our morning jobs are complete. I show Mum my diaries, Hayden shows her his scars, Dad – his laptop.

'Mum will you drop us off at school tomorrow?' Hayden asks laying in her lap as we catch up. 'I can't wait to tell my friends you are home again.'

'No,' Mum snaps, 'I can't.' Then her face dropped and she started shaking.

'Why?' he asks, sitting up off her.

As Mum sobs, Dad pulls her into his embrace. 'Your Mum and I have not worked out a way for her to legally come home.'

'I don't understand.' Hayden slid away from Mum and stood up.

I understand but I don't want to, I want to tell the whole world Mum is finally home, she loves us and didn't just run off.

'Your Mother and I are trying to work out where she may have been. Her passport has expired, there is no record of her living according to the government, bank or any other places. She has no legal footprints, so she wants to stay hidden until we know how to bring her back into reality.'

'How can we help?' I ask joining Mum and Dads with open arms.

'We will let you know when we know,' Dad promises.

After that there is a little sadness over our happy reunion. Mum gives us all her attention and wants to know all the little details about our lives that she has missed out on, soon the day is almost over, I have more to tell, more to show her and that's only our Sydney life, there is also the Pearl World to chat about. It is a part of our family now. Well, it always was we just hadn't been in on the secret.

It is almost a perfect day, we are almost a perfect family, Mum, Dad, daughter and son and I can't wait to update our family photo.

We cook bacon and egg pie together for dinner and after tea we just chat more.

By the time I am in bed my face hurts from smiling and my throat from talking too much.

Monday April 18th

Waking in my own bed, I wonder what today's champagne letters spell. I miss New Zealand but am so glad my family is together again, and not just the four of us but I have an aunty and uncle now too. Everything is great, we are safe.

I crawl out of bed and sitting on the top of my desk is an antique hat box. I take off the pearls I slept in and open the box. Inside is a bowler hat. Is it Barry's? My stomach twists, thinking of who may have put it there. I walk in to check on my brother. See if he has a new antique addition to his room. Thankfully he doesn't. I want to enjoy the bliss of having Mum with us. Not worry about Barry.

So, sticking my head in the sand like an ostrich I tuck the hat box on the top shelf of my wardrobe and behind my Winter jackets - hopefully I can forget about it for a while.

With the box tucked away out of sight, I go to wake up Hayden for the day.

'I don't want to go to school, I want to stay and get to know Mum better,' Hayden says rubbing his eyes.

'Me too,' I agree. 'We will tonight.' I see Hayden trying to hide a red notebook.

'What's that?' His face turns the colour of the cover and he swallows. 'What is it?' I ask again, this time using my motherly tone. He hands it over. It's a book of stop signs. Different colours and instructions.

'I think they are clues. I saw stop signs in some of the worlds. Did you?'

'Who knows that you have this?' I ask ignoring his question.

'You.'

'Who else?'

'Me.'

I breathe out my frustrations. 'Where did you get it?'

'It was under the shop till,' he admits.

'You just took it? Gee Hayden!' I'll have to call Aunty Claire and tell her. But first, I add the clues I remember seeing on stop signs in the worlds I visited.

'What are they?' he asks me.

'You're not the only one with secrets,' I wink before walking off to brush my teeth.

In class, I look at the chalkboard, next to it is Mr. Roundtree's antique chair...so many worlds that may be a pearl away from an adventure – maybe even treasure. Or Barry. I shudder.

At lunchtime, a group of kids are playing rugby, so I join in. They are the kids who never speak to me. But as we play, we laugh together. Just like Tama taught me. We play until the bell rings, then all chatting, we drag our feet to class.

They invite me to sit with them in maths. After school, we go to the mall and just hang out.

For what feels like the first time, I get to just be a kid.

Thoughts?

- Who is your favourite character and why?

- What was your favourite part of the book and why?

- How do you think Jellybean feels that she has to grow up quickly and help take care of Hayden?

- What board games do you think the cats were playing?

- What was your favourite world that we visited in Lavender and Pearls?

- Can you draw one of the antiques that is inside Aunty Claire's shop?

- Create your own world that you

would love Jellybean and Hayden to visit.

- What do you think happens after the story ends?

Share your thoughts and art with Sue at suecarpenterbooks@gmail.com

With Love & Thanks

All my love and thanks to.......

Love and thanks to
My family, Tonchi, Marco, Lucas, Frankie, Val, Diana and Glen for your love and support.
Janelle Andrews for your friendship, inspiration, and support always.
Elina Kivinen for mentoring me as I wrote this book.
The writers' café for critiquing a chapter of this each month.
My Auckland Writers, NZSA, Scriptorium, and IWW friends
My writing cheerleaders Anna, Cassie and Ashley.
All my friends who have put up with hours of me talking about my worlds.

Anas Jidar from Fiverr for the 1st cover design and Marly Bliss for my watercolour cover

My team Anne Carty, Melissa Gunn, Cameron Humphries and Val Carpenter
Mel from Doclans for editing
My beta readers thanks for your input.
Katie, Tramaine, Madison, Richard, Marnee, Te Maari, Amy, Anna, Melodie and Bella.
Katie and Stephen Dallow for the audio book production

Sue Carpenter

She doesn't want her readers to need a dictionary to fall into her imaginary worlds. Sue is not ready to grow up yet and keeps her mind young by writing for children and spending time with her three sons.

Instagram and Tik Tok susieleenz

www.susielee.co.nz

Puzzles and Pearls

Book two in the Pearl Saga. Just as Jellybean adjust to having her family together it unexpectedly grows but without her Magical Pearl World her new family will fall apart.

Treasure and Pearls

Book three in the Pearl Saga. Jellybean travels inside French furniture using pearls as keys. But when she, her little brother Hayden, and her best friend Austin tumble through one last world, their Pearl Magic stops working. Now they're lost in a country where no one speaks English and there are no grown-ups to help. To get home, they'll have to solve the trickiest puzzle yet. Treasures and Pearls is an adventure about family, friendship, and finding your own way.

Kaylee's Secret Mission

Still struggling from her mum's death, Kaylee is sent away from all she's ever known to move into a mansion with her father and brother she never knew. Kaylee escapes into her spy books... and then finds out that her new brother is also a sleuth fan. Together they have fun with the spy toys until she finds out their toys might be the difference between life and death. Secrets are hiding within the walls of this mansion. And Kaylee is determined to uncover them ...

Escape from the Odyssey

Ray lives for football—dribbling, shooting, scoring. He'd rather do laps around the pitch than read a book. A mysterious man wearing a white sheet plays a trick on Ray, and he gets kicked right into the pages of The Odyssey Suddenly he's battling the waves on a ship that Poseidon wants to sink.

Every time Ray survives one of Odysseus's worlds, he crash lands in a different real-life bookshelf. Ray has to keep leaping from myth to bookshop, library to myth, but will he find his way home?

The Black Manor

Belinda's uncle has taught her everything she knows about animals but when he suddenly dies, has he taught her enough to be able to run his pet business? Belinda suspects her uncle's staff are up to more than just breeding parrots so now she has to learn to care for new animals. Caged kiwis and strange sounding boxes have Belinda on edge. What secrets are the staff hiding; are her family and animals safe?

The Summer Surf

Sandra is determined to prove herself as she tries out for a summer lifesaving job – a job that will take her away from the safety of the farm into the unknown. But Sandra isn't expecting to meet someone who will change her life. She soon discovers that people can be manipulative and deceitful. Will she navigate the turbulent waters of first love and a new job.

The Dramatic Bubble

Kenzie wants to focus on her school exams with no distractions, but cupid, COVID and the government have other ideas. Will the Catholic boy be a distraction for her, or the only thing that holds her together as her family life collapses?

Blood Protectors Collection

A Dyslexic friendly, easy to read collection of short stories set in the world of the Blood Protectors.

Mosquitos who transform into beautiful tall women when they find their one chosen Blood and have to keep their Blood alive to stay alive themselves.

Sue also has a collection of picture books.